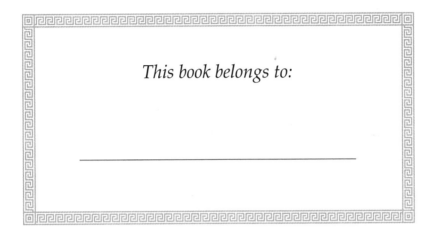

This book belongs to:

_____

YOU ARE THERE
BIBLE
ADVENTURES

Paul J. Loth

Illustrated by
Rick Incrocci

THOMAS NELSON PUBLISHERS
Nashville

Published in Nashville, Tennessee, by Oliver-Nelson Books, a division of Thomas Nelson, Inc., Publishers, and distributed in Canada by Word Communications, Ltd., Richmond, British Columbia.

The Bible version used in this publication is THE NEW KING JAMES VERSION. Copyright © 1979, 1980, 1982, Thomas Nelson, Inc., Publishers.

Printed in the United States of America.

ISBN 0-8407-9252-2

1 2 3 4 5 6 —98 97 96 95 94 93

Contents

An Open Letter to Bible Adventurers

Bible stories are exciting! The heroes of the Bible had some amazing adventures. But did you ever think about the people who shared those adventures with the Bible heroes? Who were they? What did they do?

Now is your chance to find out! This book lets *you* be a character in eight great Bible stories. You actually take part in the adventures. Plus you get to decide what happens. And each time you make a decision, the adventure changes.

Help David defeat Goliath. Help Mary and Joseph find a place to spend the night when Jesus is born. And experience a new adventure each time you enter the story. Along the way, you will get to know the Bible heroes. You will soon learn the lessons they learned long ago—God loves us and takes care of us.

Paul J. Loth, Ed.D.

Your Adventure with Jonah

—Jonah 1:1—3:10

You are a helper on a boat. In the morning you pick up passengers to go from one city to another.

You carry a lot of things, too, that people want to send to another city.

One morning people are getting on the boat. You look out at the people. You see a man wandering back and forth. He doesn't seem to know what he wants to do.

Go to page 15.

"Have a good trip!" Jonah yells.

You're embarrassed. "Never mind, go ahead," you tell the captain.

As the boat goes out into the water you look back and see Jonah still standing on the dock. He still hasn't moved from that spot. You wonder what will happen to him.

Go to page 16.

The captain stops. You hold onto the dock as Jonah runs toward you. Jonah jumps. He made it!

"OK," you yell to the captain, "you can go now." And the captain takes the boat out onto the water.

You see the land getting farther and farther away. You have a feeling this is not going to be a normal day on the water. The water already seems rough. You are beginning to get worried.

Go to page 12.

"If you say so," you tell Jonah.

You go and talk to some of your friends.

"It's worth a try," they tell you. "If we don't throw him overboard, we might all drown."

So you and your friends take Jonah and throw him over the edge of the boat.

Go to page 26.

You and all your friends on the boat start throwing all the cargo overboard. You want to make the boat as light as possible so it won't sink or tip over. Everyone is scared.

You turn around. Jonah is standing right next to you! "I knew I should have taken that boat to Nineveh. Now God is angry with me. That's why we're sinking. Throw me overboard and the storm will stop."

What should you do?

If you decide to throw Jonah overboard, turn to page 11.
If you decide to keep Jonah on the boat, turn to page 20.

"It's worth a try," your friends tell you. "If we don't throw him overboard, we might all drown."

You walk up to Jonah. "Are you sure about this?" you ask him.

"It's the only way to save the boat," Jonah says. So you and your friends pick up Jonah and throw him over the edge of the boat.

Go to page 26.

Jonah starts walking toward the boat. You stand there watching him. Your captain's strong voice interrupts your thoughts.

"C'mon, let's get going!" he yells.

You jump on the boat. The captain starts to pull the boat away from the dock.

All of a sudden, Jonah turns toward you and raises his hand. . . .

"Stop," you yell to the captain. You think Jonah might want to take your boat after all.

If you think Jonah takes your boat, turn to page 10.
If you think Jonah takes the boat to Nineveh, turn to page 9.

"Hello, sir," you say to the man. "Can I help you?"

"I'm Jonah," the man tells you. "God told me to go to Nineveh. But I don't want to go. I don't like the people there."

What should you tell Jonah?

What should you do?

If you tell Jonah he should go to Nineveh, turn to page 24.

If you tell Jonah he can go to another city on your boat, turn to page 17.

15

But there's no time to think about that now.
All of a sudden this beautiful day for sailing has become horrible.
"Throw some of this cargo overboard!" the captain yells. "We've got to keep this thing afloat."

Go to page 30.

"You don't have to go to Nineveh," you tell Jonah. "We have a boat over there that's going to another city. Why don't you come with us?"

So Jonah comes with you. You both get on the boat. Soon the boat is out on the middle of the water.

But this is not a good day to sail on the water. The water is very rough.

Go to page 12.

"Our boat is going to Nineveh," you tell Jonah. "Why don't you come with us?"

"If you don't mind," Jonah says.

"No, not at all," you say.

So Jonah gets on the boat. Soon you are out on the water on your way to Nineveh.

Go to page 31.

As you are walking around Nineveh, you notice a large crowd. Wondering what is going on, you and your friends walk over.

"God wants you to obey Him," the man is saying. "Tell Him you are sorry and that you will obey Him from now on."

As you look closer, you see that the man talking is Jonah!

People are saying that they want to obey God. They are glad Jonah came to tell them about God.

Go to page 27.

"That's ridiculous!" you tell Jonah. "This is just some rough water. God has nothing to do with it."

You keep working. But no matter how hard you and your friends try, you can't seem to steady the boat.

Go to page 23.

Jonah! . . .
You jump down from the boat.
"What happened?" you ask Jonah.
"I knew I should have taken that boat to Nineveh," Jonah tells you.
"The storm got so bad that the men on the boat threw me overboard. Then I
was swallowed by this big fish. I spent three days in that fish, and I had a lot
of time to think. I realized that we should always do what God tells us to do.
Then the fish opened his mouth and I landed here. So here I am to go to
Nineveh!"

You're fascinated by Jonah's story. But you're not so sure you want this
Jonah on your boat. He is starting to sound like bad news. And you're not
sure your friends or the captain will want him on the boat. You had a close
call last time. What should you do?

If you decide to let Jonah on the boat, turn to page 18.
If you decide to tell Jonah to take another boat, turn to page 29.

The day comes for your boat to leave.
As you are loading the boat, you look out at the people.
Whom do you suppose you see?

Go to page 21.

You turn around and see Jonah running to you. "Now what?" you think to yourself.

"I'm telling you the truth," Jonah yells. "This storm will keep getting worse until you throw me overboard."

But you just keep working.

"What did he say?" your friends ask.

"Oh, he thinks God is angry with him. He says the storm will stop if we throw him overboard."

What do you think your friends will say?

If you think your friends will want to throw Jonah overboard, turn to page 13.

If you think your friends will think Jonah is wrong, turn to page 25.

You tell Jonah he should obey God. He should go to Nineveh. "That boat over there is going to Nineveh," you tell Jonah, pointing to a boat on the other side of the dock.

Go to page 14.

"That's ridiculous," your friends tell you. "C'mon, let's get back to work."

But the storm gets worse. The boat starts tipping.

Then you hear the captain yelling. "What's going on here?" he asks you.

"This man Jonah thinks he caused this storm by disobeying God and getting on the wrong boat. And that if we throw him overboard the storm will stop. But I told him that's ridiculous."

"Not to me, it isn't!" the captain yells.

And with that he runs toward Jonah, picks him up, and throws him over the edge of the boat.

Go to page 26.

"Look out!" you call to Jonah.
You see a big fish coming to get him.
You can't believe what you see.
The fish opens his mouth and swallows Jonah.

Go to page 30.

Later, you and Jonah are sitting down together, watching the sea.

"I learned a lot about God," you say to Jonah. "I learned to obey Him no matter what. I also learned that He loves us and always wants us to have another chance to do good."

"I learned a lot about God, too," Jonah says. "A lot!"

The End.

The boat pulls away from the dock on the way to Nineveh. You explain to your friends about your conversation with Jonah.

"Wow, we're glad you told him to take another boat!" they tell you. "We've had enough exciting trips for a while."

You have a good trip to Nineveh with no problems. But you can't help but wonder what happened to Jonah.

When you arrive in Nineveh, you decide to walk around for a bit to see what's so special about this place.

Go to page 19.

"Our boat is going to Nineveh," you tell Jonah. "But I don't know if it's such a good idea for you to come along."

"Why not?" Jonah wants to know.

"Well, as you know, our last trip was kind of rocky. In fact, we wondered for a while if we were going to survive the trip or not. It might be better if you took another boat."

Go to page 28.

Right away the rough waves stop, and the water is calm.

Soon the boat arrives at the next city. You spend a few days there before the boat has to leave again.

Then the boat will be going to Nineveh. Just thinking about it reminds you of Jonah. That sends shivers up and down your spine.

Go to page 22.

All your friends are interested in finding out what happened to Jonah, too. You have a nice visit on the way to Nineveh. Jonah explains to everyone why it is important to obey God and how God took care of him.

Soon you arrive in Nineveh. "Now it's time to do the job God wants me to do," Jonah tells you.

"I'll see you later, then," you tell Jonah as he walks off.

Go to page 19.

Your Adventure with Joseph

—Genesis 37—50

You are a shepherd. You watch the sheep with other shepherds. There are some men who watch a lot of sheep. They are brothers.

Go to page 55.

You plan to tell Joseph where his brothers are, but you want to warn him first. "As you can tell, the grazing isn't real good here," you tell Joseph. "I heard your brothers say, 'Let us go to Dothan.' So they are probably there."

"Thank you," Joseph says. "I appreciate your help!"

Go to page 39.

You stand there watching as the brothers and their sheep move slowly away. It's a slow day. Not much is moving, especially your sheep. You look over the hill and see a man walking around. You'd know him anywhere. That's Joseph! You can tell from that coat of his. It is beautiful! Do you talk to him or do you mind your own business?

If you talk to Joseph, turn to page 58.
If you mind your own business, turn to page 49.

As you get near Dothan, you look up and see a group of men running toward you and yelling. "It's my brothers," Joseph tells you. He starts running toward them. But instead of talking with him, it looks like they grab Joseph and throw him in a hole somewhere. Then all the brothers walk away. After the brothers leave, you run up to the area where they threw Joseph.

Go to page 47.

His brothers must have thrown Joseph into the pit. You knew
something awful like that would happen! What should you do? Should you
try to get Joseph out of the pit? The voices are getting louder. You don't have
much time. You have to decide right away!

If you try to get Joseph out of the pit, turn to page 38.
If you leave Joseph alone, turn to page 46. But . . . you'd better hurry!

So you round up what is left of your flock and work your way toward Egypt. When you arrive in Egypt, you are told that you have to see an officer who is in charge of the King's goods. He decides who gets what. You can't believe your eyes as you walk into this large room. You'd know that officer anywhere . . . it's Joseph! Joseph tells his servants to fill your bags with food. You wonder what you should tell his brothers . . . if anything.

If you decide to tell Joseph's brothers that Joseph is in Egypt, turn to page 45.

If you go on with your life, turn to page 66.

37

You quickly look around to be sure no one is watching you. "Joseph!" you yell into the pit. "Are you all right?"

"I'm fine," Joseph calls. "I just don't understand why my brothers would want to do this to me."

Go to page 53.

"There's one more thing you should know, though," you tell Joseph, "Your brothers seemed a little angry with you when they left."

"Why was that?" Joseph asks.

"Something about a dream you told them," you explain, "and that coat your father gave you."

"Well, maybe I can explain it to them," Joseph says.

"I don't know, they seemed pretty angry," you say to Joseph. "I guess you can try."

Go to page 44.

"Can you wait a minute?" you call to Joseph. "This place is getting pretty bare. I think I'll go to Dothan, too." Joseph waits while you get all your belongings together. He helps you round up your sheep. The two of you (and the sheep) begin the walk to Dothan. Joseph tells you more about his home. He has many brothers. He also believes in God and that God knows what's best.

Go to page 35.

Before you know it, they have sold Joseph to the traders as a slave. You can hardly believe your eyes! You return to your sheep. There is nothing you can do about it now. You hope Joseph can take care of himself.

Go to page 62.

You decide to round up your sheep and move them to Dothan. As you approach Dothan you understand why Joseph's brothers came here. It is beautiful and has a lot of land for grazing.

Go to page 47.

Trying to change the subject, you say, "What do you think of this weather? It's done a good job of drying out this land."

"Have you been to Dothan lately?" the brothers ask you.

"No, I haven't," you tell them.

"We were thinking of going there. There are supposed to be good pastures for grazing there."

Go to page 34.

You watch Joseph walk away. He seems like a nice person. You hope he will be OK.

"Good luck," you yell to Joseph. Joseph stops.

"Did you say something?" Joseph asks. Do you go with him to Dothan or do you let him go by himself?

If you let him go to Dothan by himself, turn to page 61.
If you go with him to Dothan, turn to page 40.

As you leave the room, you try to remember where Joseph and his brothers lived. It has been many years since you watched your flocks together. As you are thinking about this, you notice that many people are running around excitedly. There seems to be some special news about which everyone is excited.

Go to page 54.

Just your luck, the minute you tried to get Joseph out of the pit his brothers would come by and grab you, too. You'd better stay out of it. As you're thinking about this, you hear footsteps.

"What are you doing here?" you hear Joseph's brothers ask you. "You see how we took care of our bragging brother. We'll see how he brags as a slave!" Before you can do anything, they pull Joseph out of the pit and take him to the other side of the hill.

Go to page 65.

You see a large pit ahead of you. You move your sheep over to the side. You don't want any of your sheep to fall into the pit. As you pass by you look down. Joseph's in there! Then you hear a group of men talking on the other side of the hill. You recognize those voices. They belong to Joseph's brothers.

Go to page 36.

As you keep walking you see one of Joseph's brothers. "Fancy meeting you here after all these years," you say.

"It's really something," he tells you. "We tried to do Joseph harm. But God used what we did to make Joseph important. I guess Joseph was right all along."

"How's that?" you ask.

"He always said that God had a special job for him and that he was trusting in God. I guess when we trust and obey God we can never go wrong. He will take care of us."

You remember that Joseph told you the same thing.

The End.

You try to hide from Joseph. The way his brothers sounded, you'd better stay out of it. "Shhh," you say to your sheep. You don't want Joseph to hear them. You hide behind a rock. But it's too late. Joseph has seen you already.

"Sir," he calls to you. Joseph looks up at you as you run down the hill.

"What are you seeking?" you ask him.

"I am seeking my brothers," Joseph says. "Please tell me where they are feeding their flocks."

Go to page 67.

Of course, as Joseph said, God used what his brothers did to help him. So why should he get even? "When you trust in God," you think, "there's no reason to get even with people for what they do to you." That's what Joseph would say. You're sure of that.

The End.

"You're Joseph, aren't you?" you ask him.

"Yes, I am," Joseph answers. "How did you know?"

"Because of your beautiful coat," you explain. "Your brothers were telling me about it. It is very nice."

"Then you have seen my brothers," Joseph says. "Where are they now?"

Go to page 56.

You watch Joseph walk away. He seems like a nice person. You hope he will be safe. "Good luck!" you yell to Joseph. Joseph stops.

"Did you say something?" Joseph asks.

Do you warn him about his brothers?

If you warn him, turn to page 39.

If you let him go to Dothan by himself, turn to page 61.

You're about ready to throw a rope down to Joseph. Your sheep start making a lot of noise. You wonder what is scaring them so much. As you look up, you see a line of people walking and riding camels. You know this is a group of traders. They look like they are going toward Egypt. You take a few steps to get a better look. They seem to be stopping. You wonder why.

Go to page 57.

"What's so exciting?" you ask someone as they run by you.

"Haven't you heard?" the man says. "The head officer of Pharaoh's government has just found his family. Pharaoh has given them a king's welcome. He says they have access to all the riches of Egypt!"

You can hardly believe it. It's been a strange day.

Go to page 48.

One day you are watching your sheep in a place called Shechem. You see these brothers again. They are not happy.

"What's the problem?" you ask them.

"Oh, it's our brother Joseph," they explain. "He thinks he's better than the rest of us. And you know the worst thing?"

"What's that?" you ask.

"Dad likes him best. He gave him a coat with lots of colors in it."

Go to page 43.

"They are not here," you explain.

"I can see that," Joseph says. "I want to know where they have gone."

"They didn't exactly tell me where they were going," you explain to Joseph. "All they told me was they might try another field."

Go to page 64.

You turn around to see how Joseph is doing. He is gone! You look up just in time to see Joseph being carried off with the traders to Egypt. Joseph's brothers must have sold him to the traders as a slave. You can hardly believe your eyes! You return to your sheep. There is nothing you can do about it now. You hope Joseph can take care of himself.

Go to page 62.

"What are you seeking?" you yell. Joseph looks up at you as you run down the hill.

"I am seeking my brothers," Joseph says. "Please tell me where they are feeding their flocks."

Go to page 67.

You hear a loud cry. In fact, everyone hears it. "I am Joseph, your brother," you hear Joseph say. "You meant to harm me, but God meant for me to help the people here. You shall live here with me and I will take care of you."

It is hard for you to believe. After all these years, Joseph has a chance to get even with his brothers. But he helps them instead.

Go to page 50.

You decide to tell Joseph that his brothers traveled to Dothan. The problem is between him and his brothers.

"They have departed from here. For I heard them say, 'Let us go to Dothan.'"

"Thanks a lot," Joseph says. "My father wanted me to see how they are doing."

Go to page 52.

"I said, 'Good Luck!'" you yell a little louder.

"I don't need luck," Joseph calls back, "God is going with me." You hope Joseph is right as you watch him walk out of view. You look around the pastures, now eaten over by sheep and pretty much bare. Maybe Joseph's brothers were right. Your sheep could starve at this place.

Go to page 42.

You continue to take care of your sheep. As the years go by, things are pretty good. Then all of a sudden it gets very dry. There is no rain. Your sheep get very thirsty and hungry. And the ground is very barren. It is hard to find any good ground for your sheep. You hear that Egypt is the only place to go where there are good living conditions. It can't be any worse than how you're living now.

Go to page 37.

All of a sudden Joseph announces, "Everyone out! I want to talk to these men alone!" You wonder what Joseph will do. You remember how his brothers mistreated him. You wonder whether he will be mean.

Go to page 59.

Joseph still wants to know where that new field is located. "Where is that field?" Joseph asks you. "My father wants me to see how they are doing." What are you going to tell him? Do you tell him that his brothers went to Dothan or not? Or do you tell him that his brothers were angry with him?

If you tell him that his brothers went to Dothan, turn to page 60.
If you warn Joseph that his brothers are angry with him, turn to page 33.

     You see a line of people walking and riding camels. You know this is a group of traders. They look like they are going toward Egypt. You take a few steps to get a better look. They seem to be stopping. Joseph's brothers are talking to them. You know you should do something. But what can you do to stop all those men?

Go to page 41.

You decide you should let Joseph and his brothers work out their problems. After all, it's been a long time since you have seen his brothers. You are not even sure you know where to find them. You look around the room as you are getting ready to leave. You can't believe your eyes. There are Joseph's brothers standing over there waiting to see Joseph.

Go to page 63.

You think for a moment. His brothers sounded very angry. You cannot believe Joseph would want to see them. Do you tell him that his brothers went to Dothan or not? Or do you tell him that his brothers were angry with him?

If you tell him that his brothers went to Dothan, turn to page 60.
If you do not tell him where his brothers are, turn to page 51.
If you warn Joseph that his brothers are angry, turn to page 33.

Your Adventure with Mary and Joseph

—Luke 2:1–21

You are a worker in a stable in a town called Bethlehem. The stable is filled with animals. Your job is to take care of the animals. One night you are very busy. Many, many people are arriving in town. The animals you are feeding seem nervous. "The census must be causing this," you think to yourself. Caesar Augustus told his people to return to their hometowns and be counted.

Go to page 75.

Maybe you can help find them a place to stay. The innkeeper is your friend. And you know other people in town. You do not want a pregnant woman to spend the night outside. But maybe someone else will help.

If you decide to help them find a place to stay, turn to page 83.
If you decide that they'll be all right and to let them alone, turn to page 71.

"Thank you again," Joseph tells you. You look over at Mary. She's already asleep.

"If you need anything, just let me know," you tell Joseph. You go over to check on the animals. The animals are all resting peacefully, so you decide to take a walk through the town. It has now quieted down from all the noise of the day. Mary and Joseph seem to have all they need . . . a place to rest.

Go to page 101.

You go back to work. There is still more to be done before the animals are ready for the night. As you turn around to close the doors, you see a man in the doorway. "Is this the stable?" he asks.

"Yes," you answer.

"I'm Joseph," the man tells you. "The innkeeper from across town sent me over here. You see, Mary, to whom I am engaged to be married, is expecting a child to be born any day now. We have traveled for a long time.

Go to page 95.

71

You think of your stable. It does smell, but it's warm and the hay is soft. Should you offer it to them to use for the night?

If you decide to ask Mary and Joseph if they want to stay in your stable with the animals, turn to page 100.

If you decide that it wouldn't be right, turn to page 91.

Mary and Joseph look like they need some rest. It is getting late. You wonder if you should go to bed yourself. But maybe you should stay in the stable in case Mary and Joseph need something. Mary is expecting a baby to be born soon.

If you decide to go to bed, turn to page 96.
If you decide to stay with Mary and Joseph in the stable,
    turn to page 70.

"Well, maybe I can help," you explain, "the innkeeper is a friend of mine. I know that usually he saves a couple of rooms out back. Let me see what I can do." You walk with Mary and Joseph back to the inn.

Go to page 105.

So everyone who was born in Bethlehem is returning with their families. What a mess! You've never seen so many people in all your life. And this is in a small town. No wonder the animals are so excited. You decide to take a little walk and see what is happening. This is all pretty exciting for such a little town.

Go to page 94.

You go through the door of the inn. There's a strong young man in there talking with your friend the innkeeper.

"I understand, sir," your friend is saying, "but with all these people here tonight there is just no room at all." The innkeeper greets you as you come in the room.

"How are you, friend?" he says to you.

"Not bad," you respond, "I found this fine gentleman's fiancée outside. I told her I would check to see if you had any rooms you were saving for special guests."

"I'm Joseph," the man tells you. "I see you met Mary outside. We sure appreciate your help. Mary is expecting her first child any day now."

Go to page 84.

You turn around to see a group of shepherds walking through town. They're walking in the direction of your stable. The entire town now is getting very light. The bright light is lighting up everything. The caravan is entering the town, too. And everyone is going to your stable!

Go to page 85.

"Even staying here would be fine. We are humble people."

"Well, I don't see why you can't stay here, I guess," you tell him. "It is a little smelly, but the animals are well behaved. I'm sure you'd be safe."

"That would be wonderful," Joseph says. "I'll go get Mary."

Go to page 102.

You and Joseph walk outside together.

"I'm sorry, Mary," Joseph tells his fiancée. "There is just nothing open. We tried the best we could."

"I understand," Mary says. "Don't worry. God will take care of us."

Go to page 72.

"Hello, ma'am," you call to the girl, as you walk toward her. "Are you all right?" She looks pale and very weak. She's probably just tired from the long trip.

"Yes, thank you for asking," the girl answers. She seems very nice. "I'm just tired. It's been a long trip and my fiancé and I can't find a place to stay. He's talking to the innkeeper now."

Go to page 104.

"What's going on?" you ask someone.

"Don't you know?" he says to you. "We are here to worship the new king."

"This is the king? This baby?" you ask. Joseph sees you.

"I told you this baby was special," Joseph reminds you. "This baby will be the Lord and Savior. He will save His people from their sins. And He will be king forever."

Go to page 86.

As you get ready for bed, you think about what Joseph said about this being a special baby from the Lord. You wonder what he meant by that. Soon you are asleep.

Go to page 90.

You walk out of the stable. "Hello there, again," you call to the girl riding on the donkey. You introduce yourself to them.

"I'm Mary," the girl tells you. "And this is my fiancé Joseph."

"I guess you did not have any luck at the inn," you say to them.

"No, we didn't," Joseph says. "And, as you can tell, Mary is ready to have her baby any day now."

Go to page 74.

"As I told Joseph," your friend, the innkeeper, says, "there's just nothing open. All the rooms are gone."

"But I didn't think you ever gave out all your rooms," you say.

"Normally, I don't," the innkeeper answers. "But I had no choice tonight. This place is packed with people. I'm really sorry. Don't you know of any place they can stay? Even for just one night?"

"I don't," you answer your friend. "Your inn was my best chance."

Go to page 79.

You run to your stable as fast as you can. You wonder what is
happening.

"Excuse me," you say to the people as you work your way through the
crowd. You finally get inside. You see Mary leaning against the hay, holding a
baby. She must have just had her baby! But what are all these people doing
here? People are kneeling in front of her and giving her gifts.

Go to page 81.

Now you feel bad about the stable. And He was born in a stable, your stable.

"Remember I said you were doing a wonderful thing," Mary says. "This is what God wanted. He wanted the Lord to be born in a manger in a small town with shepherds and animals and you. He's our Savior, and loves each one of us very much!"

Now you understand. That's why He's such a special baby.

The End.

"I know the innkeeper," you tell the girl. "Maybe I can talk to him about finding you a place to stay."

"That would be very nice of you," the girl tells you, "but I certainly don't want to put you to any trouble."

"No trouble at all," you assure her. "I'll see what I can find out."

Go to page 76.

You go back to work. There is still more to be done before the animals are ready for the night. As you turn around to close the doors, you see Joseph in the doorway.

"Is this where you work?" he asks.

"Yes," you answer.

"The innkeeper sent me over here," Joseph explains. "He thought you might have an idea of where we could stay tonight."

Go to page 78.

Like that girl over there sitting on the donkey. Boy she doesn't look very good. You wonder if you should see if she's all right.

If you decide to talk to her, turn to page 80.
If you decide to leave her alone, turn to page 97.

You are awakened by a bright light. It is like it's morning already. But it can't be because you just went to sleep a few minutes ago. You look out your window. You can't believe it. It looks like the entire world is at your little stable. There are shepherds and camels. It looks like someone important is down there. There are servants and a caravan of people. Probably the entire town is there. And it's the middle of the night!

Go to page 85.

"I'm really sorry," you tell Mary and Joseph. "With all the visitors these few days everything is filled."

"We understand completely," Joseph assures you. "God will take care of us." You hope Joseph is right. You say goodbye and walk back toward your stable.

Go to page 88.

When you get back to the stable you discover that your animals are all right, only still a little nervous. You continue feeding the animals and doing your chores. It's still busy outside. There are plenty of people walking around the streets. You have to look twice. That's the same girl you saw earlier. And she's with a man now.

Go to page 103.

"Is everything all right?" you ask Mary and Joseph. "Is there anything I can get for you?"

"We're fine," Joseph says. "Thank you so much. You know, this is a special baby that Mary is having. It's a gift from the Lord. God will bless you for helping us so much." You are not sure you know what Joseph means, but you thank him anyway. It still doesn't seem like such a great place to sleep. But it's better than nothing, you guess.

Go to page 73.

You go by the little inn. Normally this place is pretty crowded. But now it is mobbed. Everyone wants a room to stay for the night. But there just are not that many rooms.

Go to page 89.

"We are both very tired. There was no room in the inn. We have nowhere to go. The innkeeper thought you might have an idea. Even staying here would be fine. We are humble people."

"Well, I don't see why you can't stay here, I guess," you tell him. "It is a little smelly, but the animals are well behaved. I'm sure you'd be safe."

"That would be wonderful," Joseph says. "I'll go get Mary."

Go to page 102.

You are getting tired, you think. Maybe you should leave Mary and Joseph alone. They look very tired. They probably want to get some sleep. You check on the animals one more time. They seem all settled down for the night.

"Thank you again," Joseph tells you.

"I'll leave you alone now," you tell Joseph. "I'll check in with you in the morning. Have a good night's sleep." Mary is already asleep. She probably needs her sleep.

Go to page 82.

"She looks like she's all right," you think to yourself. "She's probably just tired." You turn around and walk back to your stable. You'd better check on your animals. They were getting pretty excited with all the people walking around. You hope they're all right.

Go to page 92.

"Well, good luck!" you say to her. "The innkeeper is a friend of mine. I'm sure that if there is a room, he'll find it for you."

Go to page 97.

"What is it?" Joseph asks.

"Well, I work in a stable," you say. "It smells a little with the animals in there. But it's warm, and the hay makes it soft."

"We'll take it," Mary and Joseph say, almost at once.

So you walk with Mary and Joseph back to the stable.

Go to page 102.

"I'm really sorry," you tell Mary and Joseph. "With all the visitors these few days everything is filled."

"We understand completely," Joseph assures you. "God will take care of us." Then you remember your stable.

"There is one other possibility," you tell them. "But I hate to even mention it."

Go to page 99.

As you walk through the town you look in the sky. Far away there is a very bright light. Almost as bright as the sun. But it's the middle of the night! And the light is moving this way. You look in the direction of the light. Way in the distance you see a caravan of camels. Just what we need, you think, more visitors to Bethlehem!

Go to page 77.

"It's nothing fancy," you tell Mary and Joseph, a little embarrassed.

"It's just fine," Mary turns to you, smiling. Joseph helps her off the donkey. You take the donkey over to an empty stall. You feed the donkey. Joseph makes a bed out of hay for Mary. She doesn't look very good. But she has a special glow that tells you there is something wonderful about to happen.

Go to page 93.

You look closer through the doors of your stable. No wonder she's not well . . . she's pregnant! They must not have been able to find a room in the inn. You're not surprised, especially with all the people here in the town tonight.

Go to page 69.

You hate the thought of this young girl spending the night outside. The innkeeper is a good friend of yours. You could probably try to get her a room.

If you talk to the innkeeper, turn to page 87.

If you decide not to talk to the innkeeper, turn to page 98.

You and Joseph walk in together.

"Well, how are you this fine night?" your friend the innkeeper greets you.

"Not bad, I must say," you answer. "But I am concerned about my friend Joseph here. His fiancée is expecting their first child. Isn't there some place they can stay, just for one night?"

Go to page 84.

Your Adventure with David and Goliath

—1 Samuel 17

You are a soldier in the Israelite army. You fight most of the battles with the army from Philistia. They are called the Philistines.

So far you have won most of the battles. But lately there has been a problem. The Philistines have a giant on their side. His name is Goliath. And he is almost ten feet tall!

Go to page 123.

"I will go with you," you tell David. You start walking with David and the king's servant. Soon you are entering the king's tent.

Go to page 120.

107

"While watching my father's sheep," David says to the king, "I killed a lion and a bear. This giant has made fun of God's armies. He will die, too." King Saul finally agrees. He probably does not have a lot of choices, you think.

Go to page 119.

"I agree, but look at the size of him!" your friend answers.

"You wouldn't want to challenge him, then?" you ask.

"No way!" your friend answers. You are about ready to try to convince your friend to fight Goliath.

Go to page 118.

"I will go with you," you call out to David. You follow him down the mountain. Goliath starts laughing as soon as he sees David coming. David stops at the brook. "I need some real smooth stones," David says to you. You help David find five stones. He puts them in his shepherd's pouch and starts walking toward Goliath. You stay by the brook and hold David's staff.

Go to page 143.

   "Well, that's true," your commander agrees, taking a minute to think about it. "All right. If you really want to do this . . . go ahead. Is there anything you need?" You take a look at your armor and your spear.

   "No, I think I have everything," you answer. Your commander walks out of his tent with you.

   "May God be with you," he says.

   Go to page 137.

You keep walking down the mountain. You hear a voice calling, "What are you doing? You're going to get yourself killed out there!" Your friends are calling you from the Israelite camp at the top of the mountain.

"You'd better listen to your friends," Goliath calls to you. "You could get killed out here! Ha! Ha! Ha!" Now you really are scared.

Go to page 130.

David walks down the mountain toward Goliath. Goliath starts laughing as soon as he sees David coming. David stops at the brook. He picks out five smooth stones and puts them in his shepherd's pouch. Then David starts walking toward Goliath.

Go to page 143.

"I need to see the king," you say to the king's servants as you approach his tent. "It is important information about the battle."

"Wait here," one of the servants tells you. He walks into the tent.

Go to page 133.

Everyone is scared of Goliath. "Well, I'm certainly not going out there," you think to yourself. You walk toward the back of the camp.

Go to page 118.

"This is not right," you think. "We're the army of the living God. We shouldn't let this giant scare us." Maybe you should go out and fight Goliath.

If you decide to go out and fight the giant, turn to page 132.
If you decide to talk another soldier into fighting, turn to page 124.
116   If you decide to be quiet, turn to page 115.

It is hard to believe a boy like this could kill a lion and a bear. But there is something about him that makes you believe him. You turn around to see a servant of King Saul walking toward you.

Go to page 136.

You hear two men arguing. "What's going on?" you ask.

"I'm David," one of the men says to you. "I came here to bring food for my brothers and to see how they were doing. Then I heard this Goliath shouting."

Go to page 127.

"Come over here," King Saul says to you. "Help this boy put on my armor." You try to get the armor on David. But he can't even walk! So David takes it all off. You can't believe that he is going to fight Goliath without any armor. But he is! "May the Lord be with you," King Saul tells David. You and David walk out of the king's tent.

Go to page 110.

"Why, he's just a little boy," the king says to you, as David walks into the tent.

"Do not fear, O King," David says. "Your servant will go and fight this Philistine."

"How can you go and fight him?" King Saul says. "You are just a boy."

Go to page 108.

Goliath is starting to look bigger! He didn't see you at first, but now he turns around.

"And what do we have here?" Just the sound of his voice makes the ground shake. You are not sure this was such a good idea now. Maybe you should return to the camp.

If you return to the camp, turn to page 130.
If you keep going to fight Goliath, turn to page 112.

You watch David and King Saul's servant walk away. You hope that King Saul is not upset about what David said. Maybe something can be done about this Goliath. God is watching over Israel, after all.

Go to page 125.

"Hey, you Israelites!" You and all the other soldiers jump as the giant calls out to you. "Send someone out to fight me! If you're not too scared that is! Ha! Ha!"

Go to page 116.

"Maybe I can get one of the other soldiers to fight Goliath," you think. You start thinking about some of the best soldiers you know. As you look around, one of your friends approaches you.

"What do you think of that guy?" he asks.

"I think someone should go down there," you answer. "He has a lot of nerve trying to take on the army of the living God."

Go to page 109.

You turn around to see David walking from the king's tent.

"What's going on?" you ask the king's servant.

"The kid here is going to fight the giant!" the servant tells you. Maybe you should go with him, you think. You could hold his staff if nothing else.

If you go with David, turn to page 110.
If you stay with the soldiers, turn to page 113.

"Who is this lad?" the king asks you.

"His name is David," you answer. "He is the brother of some of our soldiers." King Saul calls one of his servants into the tent.

"See if you can find a young boy named David," Saul tells his servant. "Tell him I want to talk with him." You wonder if you should go with the servant. You could tell David what you said to the king.

If you go with the servant, turn to page 135.
If you stay with King Saul, turn to page 129.

"I know," you tell David. "Isn't he something? Everyone is scared of him."

"Tell me," David said, "who is this man that he should challenge us? We are the people of the living God, after all."

Go to page 139.

You wonder if you should talk to King Saul about David. If the king knew that some in the army wanted to challenge Goliath and were not scared of him, maybe something could be done. Do you tell the king about David?

If you tell King Saul, turn to page 140.
If you do not tell King Saul, turn to page 134.

The servant walks out of the tent. "What else do you know about this David?" King Saul asks you.

"Not much more than I told you," you answer. "He just seems to have a real faith in the power of God." A little while later the servant walks back into the tent with David.

Go to page 120.

You turn around and run back up the mountain as fast as you can.

"Ha! Ha! Ha!" the giant Goliath yells, "I always knew you Israelites were running scared!" Your friends grab you as you get to the camp at the top of the mountain.

Go to page 142.

"No," David says to you, "the Lord did it! The battle was never ours to fight. It was God's battle. He delivered Goliath into our hands." You stop to think for a moment. God will take care of us. All we need to do is ask.

The End.

"I will fight Goliath," you decide. You try to find your commander. You want to talk to him about it.

"Do you want to talk to me?" the commander asks you.

"Yes, I do," you say. "I will go out and fight Goliath."

"Are you sure?" the commander asks.

"Yes, I don't think it is right for this Goliath to be acting this way," you answer. "God is still protecting us, isn't He?"

Go to page 111.

A minute later the servant returns.

"Follow me," he tells you. He leads you into King Saul's tent.

"What is it that you need to tell me?" Saul asks you.

"There is a young lad," you tell the king, "who is asking about Goliath. He seems special. He believes, like some of the rest of us, that God will deliver us."

Go to page 126.

David keeps talking about his belief in the living God. "This young lad sure has a lot of faith," you think to yourself. David tells you about some of his experiences while taking care of the sheep.

Go to page 117.

"Do you mind if I go with your servant, King?" you ask King Saul. "I could point David out to him."

"That is a good idea," the king says. "Go." You and the servant walk out of the tent toward the place where you last saw David. As you are walking, you tell the servant what David said. "There he is," you tell the servant when you see David.

Go to page 136.

"Excuse me. Are you David?" the servant says to David.

"Yes, I am," David says.

"The king wants to see you," the servant says. "Come with me."

Should you go with David? Maybe you can help him.

If you decide to go with David to see the king, turn to page 107.

If you decide to stay with the other soldiers, turn to page 122.

You walk out to the edge of the mountain. You look out at the giant Goliath standing below. "He doesn't look so big from up here," you think to yourself. You start walking down the mountain. You get part way down the side of the mountain and stop.

Go to page 121.

You look at the Philistines. They are running for their lives. The entire army of Israel starts to chase them. You run up to David. He is standing over Goliath. "David! David!" you say to him. "You did it! You killed Goliath!"

Go to page 131.

"I couldn't agree with you more," you tell David. There is something special about this boy, even if he is young. Some of the other soldiers are not so impressed, though. David's brothers, especially, feel that their young brother is just causing trouble.

Go to page 128.

David keeps talking to some of the other soldiers. "I'm going to tell King Saul about this young lad," you tell yourself as you walk away.

Go to page 114.

You watch David. He puts one of the stones in his sling. David runs up to Goliath . . . closer . . . closer. . . . Then David swings his sling around . . . and around . . . and sends a stone flying through the air. Right on target . . . and Goliath falls to the ground. You can't believe it. David did it! Everyone is stunned.

Go to page 138.

"Are you crazy or something?" they ask you. "What were you thinking going out there like that?" You walk to the back of the camp. "That was not smart," you think to yourself.

Go to page 118.

"You have made fun of the armies of the living God!" David shouts to Goliath. "And today God will deliver you into my hand. Then all will know that the Lord is our God." You stand amazed at this young boy's faith in God. You wish you had faith like that.

Go to page 141.

Your Adventure with Paul

—Acts 23

You are a teenager in Jerusalem. The Romans are in control of the city but the Jewish leaders are in control of the religious activities. Everyone is afraid of the high priest Ananias. He even tells the Roman soldiers what to do!

Go to page 159.

As you walk through Jerusalem you wonder what you should do next. Suddenly your thoughts are interrupted.

"What are you doing?" You look up to see your best friend, the apostle Paul's nephew, walking toward you.

Go to page 174.

You leave the barracks and say goodbye to your friend. You are amazed that Paul never said to pray for his safety. He only said to pray that he would have the courage to tell people about Jesus.

Go to page 166.

"Can we at least visit one of the prisoners?" your friend asks the guard.

"And which prisoner is that?" the guard asks.

"Paul," your friend says. "He's my uncle."

Go to page 177.

You walk with your friend to the barracks where the Romans always keep their prisoners.

"We'd like to see Paul," your friend tells the guard. The guard takes you back to see your friend's uncle. You can't believe you are actually meeting the great apostle Paul.

Go to page 155.

"Sure," you tell your friend—but he doesn't seem to be paying attention.

"Look at that over there," your friend tells you.

Go to page 182.

"I want to go see my Uncle Paul in the barracks," your friend says to you. You are not sure that's a good idea. You're just glad you're not the one in the barracks after that meeting.

If you go with your friend to see Paul in the barracks, turn to page 184.
If you go home, turn to page 163.

"What is it?" Paul asks.

"My friend and I heard some of the Jewish leaders talking," your friend says. "Ananias is planning to ask to see you again tomorrow. Then forty men will be waiting to ambush you on the way. What should we do?"

Go to page 158.

"Hurry up!" your friend says to you. "I don't want to miss this."

You follow your friend around to the back of the temple building. "This door is always open," he says to you, "but you have to be quiet." The two of you sneak into the building. You follow your friend up some stairs and look out around a pillar.

Go to page 178.

Ananias is happy to hear this. "Good for you," Ananias says. "But you know that we have tried. We are unable to condemn a man to death."

Go to page 171.

"C'mon," you say to your friend. "We need to tell your uncle about this. He needs to know what they're planning to do."

You and your friend run to the Roman barracks.

"May I help you?" the guard asks.

"I want to see Paul, my uncle," your friend tells him.

Go to page 151.

"It's nice to meet you," Paul says to you as your friend introduces you.

"My mom wanted to be sure you're all right, Uncle Paul," your friend tells Paul.

"Tell her I am fine," Paul answers. "Ask her to pray for boldness, that God will give me the courage to speak His Word."

Go to page 146.

"Someone needs to be warned about this," you say to your friend. "Let's go tell the Roman commander."

"All right," your friend agrees. "They need to know about it."

You and your friend walk over to the barracks. "We need to see the commander," your friend tells the guard.

Go to page 167.

You decide to stand outside for a while and see what happens. Soon it sounds like there is a big fight. You walk around to the back of the building where your friend entered. You are almost knocked over by a group of Roman soldiers marching out of the building. They are followed by the Jewish leaders yelling at them.

Go to page 164.

Paul calls the guard over to his cell. "Take this young man to see the commander. He has something to tell him."

You watch your friend walk away with the guard. You hope you are doing the right thing.

"The Lord came to see me last night," the apostle Paul tells you. "He told me to cheer up . . . that He would take care of me."

Go to page 169.

"C'mon, let's go!" You turn around to see one of your best friends calling to you. "My Uncle Paul is going to talk to Ananias, the high priest. I bet he'll tell the old guy off."

Go to page 172.

Before you know it, there is a big argument in the meeting. Men are standing and yelling at each other. As you turn around to leave, a group of Roman soldiers marches right by you. They grab Paul and take him away.

"Let's get out of here," you say to your friend. The two of you sneak back out of the building.

Go to page 150.

"You'll never guess what I just heard," you say to your friend.

"And what was that?"

You look around to be sure no one can hear you. "Come here," you say to your friend. You pull him over behind one of the buildings.

Go to page 179.

"Did you hear that?" your friend asks you.

"I sure did," you tell your friend. "Ananias is going to ask to see Paul, and they're going to ambush him on the way."

Go to page 188.

"I'm not going anywhere near those barracks," you tell your friend. "I almost got run over by those Roman soldiers. I'm not taking any more chances."

"My Uncle Paul has a right to see visitors," your friend tells you. "Especially members of his family."

Go to page 189.

You turn around and see your friend. "What was that all about?" you ask.

"It was great," your friend tells you. "My Uncle Paul got them arguing with each other. Pretty soon they forgot all about him. They were fighting against themselves!"

Go to page 150.

You can tell by the look in your friend's eyes that he does not understand the problem. "So?" he says to you.

"The problem is," you explain, "that there will be over forty men waiting to ambush him on his way over there!"

"Oh no!" your friend says. Now he understands the problem.

Go to page 188.

The next morning you are walking through Jerusalem. You see a number of men talking. They are right outside the building where they had the meeting with the apostle Paul. You wonder what is happening.

Go to page 175.

"No one sees the commander," the guard tells you.

"But this is an emergency," you say. "It's a matter of life and death!"

"What do you not understand?" the guard asks you. "I told you that no one can see the commander, and that is what I meant."

Go to page 147.

One of the men approaches Ananias. "We have made a promise to each other," the man says, "that we will not eat until this man Paul is dead."

Go to page 153.

You see your friend coming back. "Well, how did it go?" you ask.
"Fine," your friend says. "He will take care of it."
"The Lord will take care of it," Paul reminds you and your friend.
"That's what He promised me. All we have to do is follow Him."

The End.

"You go on ahead," you call to your friend. "Ananias gives me the creeps. You're done for if you get caught in there."

"Oh, c'mon," your friend yells back. "There's no reason to be scared."

"Just the same," you say, "I think I'll head home. I'll see you later."

"Suit yourself," your friend calls back as he runs behind the building where the meeting is being held.

Go to page 157.

The man continues talking to Ananias. "We have a plan," he says. "Tell the commander that you want to see Paul tomorrow . . . that you have more questions for him. We will be ready to jump him before he arrives."

Go to page 186.

Your friend had talked about his Uncle Paul often. His uncle had been all around the world telling people about Jesus. He had been beaten and thrown into jail many times. Almost as soon as Paul had arrived in Jerusalem, the Jewish leaders started a riot.

Go to page 180.

"Do you think it will work?" one of the men says.

"It will if Ananias can convince the commander that he really wants to talk to Paul," one of the other men says.

"Then we can jump him on the way," a third man adds. "He'll never know what hit him."

Go to page 162.

Now what should you do?

If you decide to tell your friend what you heard, turn to page 161.
If you decide to keep quiet, turn to page 185.

You try to get a little closer so you can hear without being noticed. "This Paul has got to be stopped," one of the men says.

"If we could get him out in the open away from the Romans," another man says, "we could jump him."

Go to page 187.

175

You walk around to the back of the building. You find the door that you and your friend used to sneak into the building the other day. You hide behind one of the pillars. As you look around the pillar you see a large group of men. It almost looks like the same group of men who were in the meeting with Paul the day before.

Go to page 168.

"Just a minute," the guard says to your friend. "You two wait right here."

You and your friend wait. The guard finally returns. "You two can follow me now," he tells you.

The two of you see Paul. "We have something to tell you, Uncle Paul," your friend tells the apostle Paul.

Go to page 151.

You hear a loud voice yelling. "God will strike you, you white-washed wall!"

Your friend is smiling. "That's my Uncle Paul!" he tells you. "He'll take care of Ananias."

Go to page 160.

"I heard some men talking over by that building where the Jewish Council met yesterday," you tell your friend. "They are planning to ask the Romans to bring your uncle to meet with them tomorrow."

Go to page 165.

"How are we going to get in there?" You run to catch up with your friend.

"I've sneaked in there lots of times," your friend tells you. You stop running. You have heard how Ananias feels about these private meetings. And with the Roman soldiers you are afraid of what might happen if you get caught.

If you sneak into the meeting, turn to page 152.
If you decide to go home, turn to page 170.

"So what are you doing over here?" You look up to see your best
friend, the apostle Paul's nephew, walking toward you.

"Shhhh," you say to your friend. The men start leaving the building.
You and your friend quickly hide behind a pillar.

Go to page 173.

"What?" you say.

"Those men," your friend points out. "My mom told me about them. They are nothing but trouble."

Your friend pushes you behind one of the buildings as the men walk by you.

Go to page 173.

You decide you have had enough excitement at that building. And all those men look dangerous. You decide to stay outside where it's safe.

Go to page 181.

"Well, all right," you tell your friend. "If you're sure it's all right."

"It's fine," your friend says. "You saw that meeting. My Uncle Paul's not in trouble. They're just trying to keep him safe."

Go to page 148.

"Just walking around, not doing much," you tell your friend. "Any more word from your Uncle Paul?"

"Not right now," your friend tells you. "I thought I might go over later and see how he's doing. Do you want to come along?"

Go to page 149.

You can't believe what you are hearing. You'd better leave before they see you. Now you are getting scared. You sneak out of the building.

Go to page 145.

Soon all the men walk into the building. You wonder what they are planning to do. You wonder if you should follow them into the building.

If you decide to follow, turn to page 176.
If you decide to stay outside, turn to page 183.

"What should we do about it?" your friend asks you.
You wonder if you should talk to the Roman commander about it.

If you decide to talk to the Roman commander, turn to page 156.
If you decide to warn the apostle Paul, turn to page 154.

"You might be right," you tell your friend. "But I'm going home just the same. I've had enough excitement for one day."

"If you wish," your friend says. "I'll see you tomorrow, then."

You say goodbye to your friend and head home.

Go to page 166.

Your Adventure with Baby Moses

—Exodus 1:15—2:10

Your mother is a midwife in Egypt. It is her job to help Jewish mothers when they have babies. The mothers talk about God. They say that God will take care of them.

Go to page 202.

"Look at her holding your baby brother," you tell Miriam. "I don't think she is going to hurt him. Maybe you could offer to have your mother take care of the baby for her."

You and Miriam walk down to where Pharaoh's daughter is holding the baby.

Go to page 228.

"It's too dangerous," you tell the woman. "We've tried to help you. We've let you keep the baby here. But I could be in trouble if they found me carrying the baby down to the river like this. Besides, someone might find the baby down there. I just don't think it's a good idea."

Go to page 225.

"Hello," the king's daughter says as she walks by you.

"Nice day, isn't it?" you say.

"Yes, very nice."

You follow her to the edge of the river. "My mom has been washing dirty clothes here," you tell her. "Why don't you wash in another part of the river today?"

Go to page 223.

"He really is beautiful," you tell the boy's mother.

"There's something special about this baby," the woman tells you. "I know it's dangerous, but I'm going to keep him."

Go to page 211.

"Ma'am!" you call to the king's daughter.

"Yes?" she says.

You're not sure what to say next. You only know you need to do something. You hear someone behind you.

"Could . . . could I get a Jewish woman to take care of the baby for you?"

Go to page 217.

You tell your mom, "God is really taking care of us."

But the Egyptian king, Pharaoh, is getting worried. One day your mom goes to a meeting with the king.

Go to page 230.

"What's the problem?" the woman asks you.

"The king's daughter has found your baby!" you explain. "Hurry!"

You and the baby's mother run down to the river. You are almost there when the woman stops. "Look," she says.

Go to page 233.

Miriam runs to get her mother. Soon the baby's real mother comes down the hill to the river. You stand with Miriam as you watch Pharaoh's daughter give the baby back to his real mother.

"I was just thinking about what your mother said earlier," you say to Miriam.

Go to page 220.

"All right, I'll help you," you tell the woman. "I just hope you are not making a big mistake."

"God will keep him safe," the baby's mother tells you. "And He will bless us, too, for obeying Him."

Go to page 232.

"I know," the baby's mother says to your mom, "but he's such a beautiful baby."

"I can hide him in my house for you," your mom finally agrees. "But only for three months."

"That's wonderful," the baby's mother says. "God will bless you for this."

Go to page 207.

As you leave the woman's house, you wonder if the baby will be all right.

You go down by the river. Soon the woman and her daughter, Miriam, walk out of their house carrying the basket. Quietly they place the basket on the edge of the river.

Go to page 235.

Many of the Egyptian women do not have a lot of children. But the Jewish women keep having more and more children. And the children live. They do not die like many of the Egyptian children. Pretty soon there will be more Jewish people than Egyptian people.

Go to page 196.

"Could . . . could I get a Jewish woman to take care of the baby for you?" Miriam asks.

You stand amazed at this little girl. God must have told her what to say. She said just the right thing.

"Yes, that would be very nice," the king's daughter says.

Go to page 198.

You wonder if you should try to stop her from getting too close to the basket.

If you try to stop her from washing in the river, turn to page 214.
If you try to get her to go to another part of the river, turn to page 193.
If you decide to leave the king's daughter alone, turn to page 209.

You know that if you are seen with this baby boy you will be in big trouble. But you feel sorry for this woman. And there is something special about this baby.

If you take the baby down to the river, turn to page 199.
If you try to talk the woman out of it, turn to page 208.
If you leave the woman's house without helping her, turn to page 192.

205

"Could you take a look at something over here, ma'am?" you say to Pharaoh's daughter, trying to keep her away from the river.

"Well, just for a minute," she says to you.

Go to page 223.

Every day for three months, the woman comes over to your house to check on the baby and to help you and your mom take care of him.

Go to page 221.

"Are you sure that is a good idea?" you ask the woman. You are afraid the baby will not be safe. "A lot can happen to a baby down by the river."

"I know," the woman agrees, "but Miriam will be watching him. And God will protect him."

Go to page 199.

You decide to leave the king's daughter alone. She might think you were trying to hide something from her and start looking around.

"Hello," she says as she walks by you.

"Nice day, isn't it?" you say.

"Yes, very nice."

Now you're starting to get nervous.

Go to page 226.

You start running up the hill as fast as you can. You have to find the baby's mother.

You run to the woman's house. She is standing outside. "You have to come quickly!" you say to the woman.

Go to page 197.

"Are you sure you want to do that?" your mom asks the woman. "You know what Pharaoh said."

"Yes, I know," the woman tells you. "But God will protect me . . . and my baby."

Every day for three months, you and your mom sneak over to the woman's home to check on her and the baby. Your mom gives you baby clothes to take over to the woman.

Go to page 218.

You think for a moment. You look down at Pharaoh's daughter. You can't believe what you see. She is holding the baby in her arms. She must have seen how beautiful he is, too.

Go to page 219.

Your mom asks you what she should do. She should not go against God. But she is afraid to disobey the king, too.

Go to page 222.

"Hello," the king's daughter says as she walks by you.
"Nice day, isn't it?" you say.
"Yes, very nice."

Go to page 206.

"So what do you want to do?" you ask the woman.

"Put the baby in this basket," she tells you. "Then take it down to the river. Hide my baby there. My older daughter, Miriam, will watch him."

Go to page 224.

"Are you ready for me to take him now?" you ask the woman.

"There's something special about this baby," the woman tells you. "I don't want to give him up."

"But you know what the king's orders are," your mom tells her.

Go to page 200.

You turn around. It's Miriam. She must have seen the king's daughter take her baby brother.

"Yes," Pharaoh's daughter says. "That would be wonderful."

You take Miriam aside. "What are you going to do?"

"I'm going to get my mother," Miriam tells you.

Go to page 198.

One day, you stop to visit the baby's mother. You see her preparing a basket. You ask her what she is doing. "I can't hide my son in this house any longer," she tells you. "I'm afraid we're going to get caught."

Go to page 227.

The thought comes to you . . . maybe the king's daughter would want someone to take care of the baby for her. The baby's real mother could do that.

If you tell Miriam to ask Pharaoh's daughter, turn to page 191.
If you tell Miriam to tell the king's daughter that she is the baby's sister and the baby belongs to her, turn to page 231.

"What was that?" she asks you.

"About how God would keep your baby brother safe," you answer. "Only a great God could have worked all this out so well. God really does take care of everything if we let Him."

The End.

One day, when she stops to visit the baby, she is carrying a basket. You ask her what she is doing. "I can't hide my son in this house any longer," she tells you. "I'm afraid we're going to get caught."

Go to page 215.

One day a woman has a beautiful baby boy. You help your mom take the baby and wrap him in warm clothes. "Here's your baby," you tell the woman.

Go to page 229.

You're proud of yourself for getting the king's daughter to leave the area where the baby is floating in the basket. But as she walks away from the river she sees the basket.

Go to page 226.

You know that if you are seen with this baby boy you will be in big trouble. But you feel sorry for this woman. And there is something special about this baby.

If you take the baby down to the river, turn to page 199.
If you try to talk her out of it, turn to page 208.

"I understand," the woman tells you. "Thank you for all your help."
You feel sorry for her.

"If you do put the baby in the river," you tell her, "I will help watch your baby."

"Thank you," the woman tells you. "That would be wonderful. God will protect us all. He will keep my baby safe."

Go to page 201.

"Look over there!" the king's daughter shouts as she points to the basket. Your heart skips a beat. You knew this would happen. Should you go and tell Miriam what is happening? Or should you try to save the baby before anything happens to him?

If you decide to tell Miriam, turn to page 234.
If you decide to try to save the baby on your own, turn to page 195.
If you decide to run and get the mother, turn to page 210.

"So what are you going to do?" you ask the woman.

"I am putting my baby in this basket," she tells you. "Please take it down to the river. Hide my baby there. My older daughter, Miriam, will watch him there."

Go to page 205.

"Could I get a Jewish woman to take care of the baby for you?" Miriam asks the king's daughter.

"Yes, that would be very nice," the king's daughter says.

Go to page 198.

"He's beautiful," the woman says, holding him in her arms. As you watch the woman hold her baby boy, you wonder what your mom will do. You know the king's orders. This is a baby boy. But you know your mom does not want to disobey God.

If you let the woman keep her baby, turn to page 194.
If you take the baby away from the woman, turn to page 216.

"There are too many Jewish babies being born," Pharaoh tells her. "Soon they will be stronger than the Egyptians. Only save the girl babies. Do not save the boy babies."

Go to page 213.

"Go down there right away," you say to Miriam. "Tell her that the baby belongs to you. Then she'll have to give him to you."

You and Miriam run down the hill. "Ma'am," Miriam says to the king's daughter.

"Yes?" King Pharaoh's daughter says. You look at her holding the baby. She really seems to like him.

Go to page 203.

231

You look around to be sure no one is watching as you leave with the basket. You and Miriam quietly walk down to the river. You place the basket in a safe spot near the edge of the river.

Go to page 235.

You see Miriam talking to Pharaoh's daughter. You keep going down to the river. You can almost hear what she is saying.

"Could I get a Jewish woman to take care of the baby for you?" Miriam is asking.

"Yes, that would be very nice," the king's daughter says.

Go to page 198.

"Hurry! Hurry!" you call to Miriam as you run up the hill. "There's trouble. We need to do something right away!"

"What should we do?" Miriam asks you.

Go to page 212.

You try to keep an eye on the basket as you do your work. You notice that Miriam is watching, too.

You hear someone coming. It's a group of women. "Oh no," you think to yourself. "It's the king's daughter!" You know she often washes herself in the river.

Go to page 204.

Your Adventure with Jesus and the Disciples

—Matthew 8:23–27; Mark 4:35–41; Luke 8:22–25

You are a fisherman on the Sea of Galilee. You enjoy fishing. You have made many good friends fishing. You spend many hours in a fishing boat. Sometimes you have spent all night fishing with your friends. Then you bring your fish to shore first thing in the morning. That is when you sell them in the market.

Go to page 248.

"No, not really," you say to Jesus. So Jesus explains the story to you. It seems simple when He explains it. You do not know why you did not understand it before.

Go to page 253.

"Great," Simon says. Jesus turns to you.

"Thank you very much," Jesus says to you. "You are very kind." Jesus gets in the boat. You decide to listen as you keep working on your nets.

Go to page 256.

You cannot understand how someone can sleep through all this. You wonder if you should wake Him. Maybe He can help. He seems to have the answer to every other problem.

If you wake Jesus, turn to page 252.
If you let Jesus sleep, turn to page 263.

After Jesus has finished talking, Simon helps you put your nets back in the boat.

"Did you understand what Jesus was saying?" you ask Simon.

Go to page 251.

"I'm going to wake the Lord!" Simon yells to you. "How can He sleep at a time like this?"

Go to page 246.

You notice that you do not see Jesus. "Where's Jesus?" you ask Simon. You wonder if something has happened to Him.

"He's here in the back of the boat!" one of the other disciples yells back. "He's sleeping."

Go to page 261.

You're still having trouble keeping the boat from tipping over. Jesus holds onto the rail on the outside of the boat. He looks out over the water. The water almost covers Jesus as He holds out His hand.

"Peace!" Jesus shouts out from the boat. "Be still!"

Go to page 267.

"How can He sleep at a time like this?" you ask Simon. "We could all die! Doesn't He care?"

Go to page 246.

You feel bad now. After all, you were the one who put Simon up to it.
"I'm sorry, Simon," you say. "I hope I didn't get you in trouble. Who is this Jesus anyhow? Even the wind and the waves obey Him!"

Go to page 249.

You and Simon run to where Jesus is sleeping. You shake Jesus awake. "Don't You care that we are all dying?" Simon asks Jesus.

Go to page 268.

Should you let Jesus teach them from your boat?

If you let Jesus get in your boat, turn to page 278.
If you keep working on your nets, turn to page 254.
If you decide to leave, turn to page 270.

One morning you bring your boat into the shore. You are cleaning your nets and talking with some of your friends. One of your best friends is Simon Peter. He is a big fellow. You can hear Simon for miles around. Everyone likes him. However, Simon has not been around the fishing boats lately. You wonder what has happened to him.

Go to page 262.

You have been through many scary times on the sea with Simon. He is one of the toughest seamen you know. You have never seen the look in his eyes you see right now.

"He's the One for whom we have been waiting," Simon tells you. "We have nothing to fear if we are with Him. He will always take care of us." You know you will never forget this day. It is the day you met Jesus.

The End.

"I'm going to wake the Lord!" Simon yells to you. "How can He sleep at a time like this?"

Go to page 259.

"The parables, you mean?" Simon asks you.

"Yes, those stories," you say to Simon.

"Not all of them," Simon tells you. "Many times the Lord will explain them to us later. Why don't you ask Him?"

Go to page 276.

"As long as He's all right," you yell to Simon. You go back to work. You have to save the boat. But the storm only gets worse. Now water has filled up almost half the boat. You can feel the boat going down a little into the water. For the first time you are starting to get a little scared.

"I'm going to wake the Lord," Simon yells to the other disciples. "How can He sleep at a time like this?"

Go to page 259.

It is almost evening now. Most of the people have started to go home.

"Let us cross over to the other side of the lake," Jesus says. You really need to get back to work. Should you go out on the lake, too?

If you go out on the lake, turn to page 271.

If you stay at the shore, turn to page 269.

253

You go back to working on your nets. As you are cleaning the nets, you notice several spots that need to be repaired. You have a lot of work to do before you go out on the boat again. The people are still crowding in on Jesus. They are not leaving you much room to work on your nets, either. You look up and see Jesus sitting in Simon's fishing boat, talking to everyone.

Go to page 256.

You have been through many scary times on the sea with Simon. He is one of the toughest seamen you know. You have never seen the look in his eyes you see right now.

"He's the One for whom we have been waiting," Simon tells you. "We have nothing to fear if we are with Him. He will always take care of us." You know you will never forget this day. It is the day you met Jesus.

The End.

Jesus is telling stories to the people. You are not sure you understand what the stories really mean. Most of the people look confused, too.

Go to page 240.

Immediately the storm stops. You have never seen anything like that. It's almost scary. The storm did what Jesus told it to do! Jesus looked at the disciples.

"Why were you so worried?" Jesus asks them. "Do you still not have any faith?"

Go to page 245.

"It sure is getting windy," you say to Simon. You try to steady the boat. Pretty soon the waves are getting so high that water is splashing into the boat. You and Simon try everything to steady the boat. Some of the other disciples of Jesus are trying their best to steady the boat, too. Nothing seems to work. In fact, it seems like the boat is tipping more. There is more water in the boat than before. You wonder if you are going to tip over.

Go to page 242.

Simon and some of the other disciples run to where Jesus is sleeping. They shake Jesus awake. "Don't You care that we are all dying?" Simon asks Jesus.

Go to page 277.

You return from your walk a few hours later. It is getting near evening now. You start working on your nets again.

Go to page 266.

You cannot understand how someone can sleep through all this. You wonder if you should wake Him. Maybe He can help. He seems to have the answer to every other problem.

If you wake Jesus, turn to page 244.
If you let Jesus sleep, turn to page 265.

As you look around, there's Simon. He is talking to that man Jesus. You have heard a lot about Him. "Hey, Simon!" you call to your friend. "Haven't seen you around much lately!"

Go to page 272.

"As long as He's all right," you yell to Simon and go back to work. You have to save your boat. But the storm only gets worse. Now water has filled up almost half the boat. You can feel the boat going down a little into the water. For the first time you are starting to get a little scared.

Go to page 250.

"It's good to meet you," Jesus says to you. He shakes your hand. There is something about Jesus that makes you like Him right away. A large crowd is gathering now. There is no room for anyone to stand. Everyone is crowding in on Jesus, trying to get close to Him.

Go to page 247.

"As long as He's all right," you yell to Simon and go back to work. You and Simon have to save the boat. But the storm only gets worse. Now water has filled up almost half the boat. You can feel the boat going down a little into the water. For the first time you are starting to get a little scared.

Go to page 241.

You check out your nets. You want to try fishing one more time today before you quit.

Your nets are ready for another big catch. So you start out to your favorite fishing area on the lake. "It seems like it is getting dark," you think to yourself. Soon you feel a few raindrops. The boat starts tipping one way . . . then another. You try to keep the boat afloat.

Go to page 273.

Immediately the storm stops. You have never seen anything like that. It's almost scary. The storm did what Jesus told it to do! Jesus looks at the disciples.

"Why were you so worried?" Jesus says to them. "Do you still not have any faith?"

Go to page 275.

Jesus looks up at the storm. It doesn't even seem to worry Him. In all the years of being out on the sea, you have never seen someone so calm during a storm. Jesus looks at Simon. It is almost as if Simon had no reason to be so scared!

Go to page 243.

"Thank you very much for the use of your boat," Jesus says to you. Jesus and His disciples get in Simon's boat and start out across the lake.

Go to page 266.

You try to keep working on your fishing nets but it is getting crowded. So you decide to take a walk. You have been working hard lately. You can use the break.

Go to page 260.

"You can go in my boat, Jesus," you tell Jesus.
"If that's not a problem, great," Jesus tells you.

Go to page 274.

"I've been with Jesus," Simon tells you. He introduces you to Jesus. By now a crowd is starting to gather.

Go to page 264.

As you look out over the lake you see several other boats all fighting to stay afloat. The waves are so high water is filling up all the boats. You look closer at the boat next to you. It's Simon!

"Are you all right, Simon?" you yell. You and Simon have been through many tough battles on this sea.

"We're doing our best!" Simon yells back.

Go to page 279.

"Not at all," you say to Him. "I need to get to the other side of the lake anyway." You, Simon, and Jesus, along with some of the other disciples, push away from the shore in your boat. You and Simon have a great time talking together on the boat. It seems like old times. You don't even notice that it is getting dark and windy.

Go to page 258.

You feel bad now. After all, you were the one to put Simon up to it. "I'm sorry, Simon," you say. "I hope I didn't get you in trouble. Who is this Jesus anyhow? Even the wind and the waves obey Him!"

Go to page 255.

"Lord," Simon says to Jesus, "my friend here has a question."

"And what is that?" Jesus asks you.

"Why do you tell stories to the people?" you ask Jesus.

"My followers," Jesus says, "understand the things of God. But those on the outside are only told parables. Don't you understand this parable?"

Go to page 237.

Jesus looks up at the storm. It doesn't even seem to worry Him. In all the years of being out on the sea, you have never seen someone so calm during a storm. You're still having trouble keeping your boat from tipping over. Jesus holds onto the rail on the outside of the boat. He looks out over the water. The water almost covers Jesus as He holds out His hand.

"Peace!" Jesus shouts out from the boat. "Be still!"

Go to page 257.

"Simon," you call to your friend, "there's no room on the shore here. Your friend, Jesus, can talk to the people from my boat if He wants."

Go to page 238.

You notice that you do not see Jesus. "Where's Jesus?" you ask Simon. You wonder if something has happened to Him.

"He's here in the back of the boat," one of the other disciples yells back. "He's sleeping."

Go to page 239.

Your Adventure with Jesus and the Paralyzed Man

—Mark 2:1–12

You live in Capernaum. One of your best friends when you were growing up was Jesus. At that time you remember Him as a carpenter. His father, Joseph, was the carpenter in town. You and Jesus would spend time together building things.

Go to page 294.

You and Jesus soon decide to go to sleep.

You are awakened by the sound of people talking. The more you listen, the more people you hear! You look out your window. You see crowds and crowds of people standing outside. They are waiting to get into your house. They must have heard that Jesus was staying with you!

Go to page 298.

The men carry their friend and follow you behind the house. You watch with amazement as the four men somehow get their friend up the ladder and onto the roof.

Go to page 295.

"Jesus probably knows that he wants to be healed," you think to yourself.

Go to page 285.

A couple of people turn around to look. But still there is not enough room to get through.

"I *am* sorry," you say to the men. "I knew it would be difficult."

Go to page 299.

Jesus looks in the direction of those religious leaders. "Why are you thinking like that? What is easier? To tell someone his sins are forgiven or to tell him to rise and walk?" Jesus asks them.

These religious leaders are tongue-tied. They can't say a thing.

Go to page 314.

"Oh, that's nice," your friend says. "Well, have a good time."
"I will," you answer. "Maybe some other time."
"Great," your friend says. "Goodbye."
As your friend leaves, you go back to talking to Jesus.

Go to page 281.

Some of the tile from the roof falls down by Jesus' feet as you make an opening in your roof.

"Excuse us!" you shout, as more pieces of the roof tile fall into the room by Jesus. You help the men lower their friend to Jesus' feet. You wait to see Jesus heal the man. That's what the man wants.

Go to page 303.

You think for a moment. You have seen people move pieces of the roof around. You wonder if the men could get in to see Jesus that way.

If you offer to let them climb through your roof, turn to page 307.
If you tell them no, turn to page 292.

The crowd gets louder and louder. "You'd have to be crazy to let that mob into your house," you think to yourself. "They'd tear the place apart!"

Go to page 302.

"May I help you?" you ask the men as they approach your house.

"We need to see Jesus," the men say to you. "Our friend here is paralyzed. We know Jesus can help him."

Go to page 313.

The four men carrying the paralyzed man aren't sure that is a good idea.

But the paralyzed man on the mat thinks it's great. "Let's do it!" he shouts to his friends.

"I have a ladder and some rope in the back of the house," you say to the men. "You'll need the rope to lower your friend down from the roof."

Go to page 282.

"I'm sorry," you try to explain to the man. "This is the only entrance. There is just no way to get in to see Jesus. Maybe you could come back later when there aren't so many people here. . . ."

"How about the roof?" the paralyzed man interrupts you.

"What?" you and his friends ask at the same time.

"The roof!" the man says again. "What if we remove some roof tiles? You can lower me down to Jesus that way."

Go to page 300.

"I'm sorry," you say to the men. "I understand how you feel. But there is just no way anyone can get in there. *I* can't even get in there . . . and it's my house!"

Go to page 299.

Even then you could tell that Jesus was special. He always seemed more serious than the rest of your friends. And He always had the right word to say to help people with their problems.

Now you know why Jesus was so special. He is the Messiah! People follow Jesus everywhere He goes. But Jesus has never forgotten you. Every time He is in town, He stops to see you.

Go to page 315.

All of a sudden you see the crowd back away from the center of the house.

"Excuse us!" one of the men shouts as pieces of the roof tile fall into the room by Jesus. You can see the men lower their friend to Jesus' feet. You wait to see Jesus heal the man. That's what the man wants.

Go to page 311.

You wonder if you should tell your friend that it is Jesus. You know Jesus could use the rest. He does look tired.

If you tell your friend it is Jesus, turn to page 308.
If you keep quiet about Jesus' being in your house, turn to page 286.

"Jesus!" you shout down through the roof. But Jesus doesn't hear you.

Go to page 285.

If you let them in, you're afraid they might destroy your home. But you can't just leave them outside, either.

If you decide to let them come into your house, turn to page 306.
If you decide to leave them outside, turn to page 289.

"Well, we tried," the men say as they turn to walk away.

"Wait a minute," the paralyzed man says. "Isn't there a back entrance to your house or a window? I know Jesus could help me if I could just get in to see Him!"

Go to page 288.

"Well, I guess that would work," you agree. "I have a ladder and some rope in the back of the house," you say to the men. "You'll need the rope to lower your friend down from the roof."

The men carry their friend and follow you behind the house. You help the four men somehow get their friend up the ladder and onto the roof.

Go to page 287.

A few people try to move over a little bit. But even then there is no room to get into the house. You decide to try again.

"There is a paralyzed man back here who needs to see Jesus," you call out to the crowd.

Go to page 284.

Soon the noise seems to be quieter. You only hear one voice now. It's Jesus talking! You walk out to the room where Jesus was sleeping. Everyone is listening to Him. They don't seem nearly as wild as they sounded before. You walk through the crowd to the outside of the house.

Go to page 317.

But your friend, Jesus, is always full of surprises. "Your sins are forgiven!" Jesus says to the man on the mat.

You wonder if you should explain to Jesus that the man wants to be healed. Maybe Jesus does not know that.

If you decide to ask Jesus to heal the man, turn to page 297.

If you decide that Jesus doesn't need your help, turn to page 283.

As you are thinking about this, you see several men walking toward you. They are carrying a man lying on a mat. Probably someone else for Jesus to heal. You wonder how they think they are going to get in to see Jesus.

Go to page 290.

His friends are still on your roof. They start cheering! They jump off the roof and meet him outside your house.

"What did I tell you?" the man said to his friends as they walk away. "I told you Jesus could do it. He can do anything! He's God's Son!"

Go to page 312.

You walk toward the door. You see Jesus just waking up, too. "I think we have some visitors," you tell Jesus. "You don't mind if I let them in, do you?"

"That's fine," Jesus answers. "As I said, they are the ones I came to serve."

You open the door about two seconds before the people break it down.

You almost get knocked over as the people charge into your house. Many have questions for Jesus and some people want Jesus to heal them. But all of the people want to listen to Jesus.

Go to page 317.

"There is one possibility," you say to the men. The face of the sick man brightens. "I do know that the tiles on these roofs can be easily removed. If you can get up there, maybe you can lower your friend through the roof down to Jesus."

Go to page 291.

"I think you probably know Him," you say as you open the door wider. "You know Jesus, don't you?"

Jesus gets up and comes to the door. Your friend is stunned. He did not know Jesus was staying with you. You are already wondering if introducing your friend to Jesus was the right thing to do. You are afraid that soon the entire town will know.

Go to page 320.

You wave at Jesus. He doesn't see you at first, so you keep waving. When Jesus looks up at you, He can see you're upset. You point at the religious leaders standing in front of you. Jesus looks at you as if to say, "I know. I know what they're thinking."

You start to wonder, "How does He know what they're thinking?"

Go to page 285.

You feel sorry for the poor man. But you don't know how to get him in through the crowd. Do you help him get in to Jesus, or do you tell them to go home?

If you try to help the men, turn to page 318.

 If you tell the men to go home, turn to page 293.

But your friend, Jesus, is always full of surprises. "Your sins are forgiven!" Jesus says to the man on the mat.

The men from the temple standing right in front of you are furious. "He has no right to do that!" they whisper to each other. You wonder if you should tell Jesus what they said.

If you decide to tell Jesus, turn to page 309.
If you decide to keep quiet, turn to page 319.

The man's words ring in your ears as you look back at Jesus. That's why Jesus was always different. He *is* God's Son and He's *your* friend. What a great privilege . . . to be friends with the Son of God and to know that Jesus cares about you!

The End.

"Well, this is my house," you explain. "As you can see it is very crowded. There doesn't seem to be a very good chance to get in there to see Him."

"There has to be a way," the men say. "This is our friend's only chance. Can't you please help him?"

Go to page 310.

313

So Jesus keeps talking. "To prove to you that the Son of Man has the right to forgive sins, I say to you stand up, pick up your mat, and go home!"

Go to page 316.

Jesus is staying with you one night. You are having a wonderful time. You think back over the good times you had as teenagers. Soon there is a knock on the door.

"Can you come over tonight?" one of your friends asks you.

"Not tonight," you answer. "I have a friend from out of town staying over tonight."

Go to page 296.

You've known Jesus a long time but you've never seen anything like this. This man stands up in front of everyone and picks up his mat and walks out of your house. Everyone moves out of his way *now*!

Go to page 305.

As you look around the crowd, you notice a strange group of men standing right outside your house. (There is no room for anyone inside the house anymore.) You have seen these men somewhere before. They are the leaders in the temple. These are the men who keep giving Jesus trouble everywhere He goes. Jesus was telling you about these people last night. You wonder what they are doing here.

Go to page 304.

"Well, maybe I could ask some of these people to move so we could get in to see Jesus," you tell the men.

"That would be great," the men say.

They pick up the man lying on the mat as you try to find an opening in the crowd.

"Excuse me," you say to some people. "Excuse me. I live here. Could I get into my house please?"

Go to page 301.

"What Jesus doesn't know can't hurt Him," you think to yourself. "He's had enough problems with this group already."

Go to page 285.

"I'm afraid that was a mistake," you say to Jesus as your friend leaves.
"Why is that?" Jesus asks you.

"Because I'm afraid the entire town will soon know that You are here," you answer. "My friend is not known for keeping secrets."

"I understand," Jesus says, "but do not worry. Those are the people for whom I came."

Go to page 281.